The Complete Collection
of people, places & things

John Dermot Woods

BlazeVOX [books]
Buffalo, New York

The Complete Collection of people, places and things
by John Dermot Woods

Published by BlazeVOX [books]

© creative
commons
Creative Commons License:
Attribution-Noncommercial-Share Alike

Printed in the United States of America

Book design by Geoffrey Gatza

First Edition
ISBN: 9781935402466
Library of Congress Control Number 2009925622

BlazeVOX [books]
14 Tremaine Ave
Kenmore, NY 14217

Editor@blazevox.org

publisher of weird little books

BlazeVOX [books]

blazevox.org

for all the Francis James Woodses

ITEMS

By remembering it I have been able to understand many people and things that I was never able to understand before.

—SHERWOOD ANDERSON
WINESBURG, OHIO

The
Complete
Collection
of people, places & things

A Village Beyond Approach

THE COLLECTOR, an aging man who smoked short, fat cigarettes, broke his pen nibs much more often than he should have. They were all gifts and made of gold, a very soft metal. A young man—who drank his coffee in slurps and broadcasted his opinions loudly—saw the collector struggling mightily with his broken pen. The brash youth offered him a box of ballpoints, erasables. After all, the collector needed to transcribe the world around him, and a broken pen shouldn't be enough to stop his work—which was the actual creation (not recording) of posterity.

The collector scrawled a few shapes with his new disposable pen and spoke to the young man beside him. He lit a cigarette, a signal that he was taking a break from his writing. They talked about history and who could create it.

The collector admitted that there were times his pen lost the shape of the world he intended to craft. He was once a part of a league (he thinks it was organized by the local Policemen's Benevolent Association). It was a whole collection of collectors who pooled their efforts. They compared, contrasted, refined, and traded their doubles. But, over the years, trends kept changing, and, as such, the process of transcribing history became more taxing. Most of his compatriots found more ephemeral subjects to collect and quickly discard. When he was left alone, his words faltered and he fell silent. He stabbed his new pen at an empty page, piercing his notebook ten pages deep. The young man couldn't bear an unstable collector, and he took his pens back.

The collector watched the stars glittering on the cover of his shut notebook. He picked it up and wrung it tight. The young man took that too. It was too valuable to lose. The collector smoked four more cigarettes, then threw away the rest of the pack. Right then, he understood the history he had created. *For the first time,* he told the loud young man. He needed his notebook back; he needed his story. He needed to set it straight. The young man obliged.

The collector began all over again, and he scratched out the world as he thought it should be understood. He claimed this work was a *culmination.* When he was done, his companion was still beside him. *This is the final record of our time,* the collector said. *It can no longer be approached.* He gave the notebook to the young man, but said he'd like to keep the box of ballpoints, should anything else strike him.

I saw the notebooks only once. It wasn't just a recounting, or some sort of a Manual; it was complete. As he was seized by the frenzy to acquire history, I don't know that the collector ever understood that his goal was fully realized. I don't remember it all, but I do remember that it was completely focused. He thought he was creating the whole world, but, as I read it, it was clearly his own world. It could not have been anything but a re-creation of his home—a much more valuable resource than the project he had intended. I can't visit that town, but I can see it in my own. I see pieces of my world that I thought would be forever hidden.

It was the complete reality of his accounts that made them so unapproachable. His descriptions were ultimately comprehensive; his world was one that left no luxury for erosion. Its reality was certainly what prevented his notebooks from being printed (and reprinted). The book only lives on in my flawed memory and the memory of the others of my time who had the opportunity to read his hand-scrawled notes.

The young man accepted the collector's writings, each and every notebook that he had filled on the bench that day, and then he reclaimed his box of erasable pens, as the collector wanted to keep going, filled with a lust to gather. But the young man told him that history had been complete and he refused to let the collector change a thing.

*

Here I can only report his wholeness with my own imperfect recall.

Optimus Prime

OPTIMUS PRIME SWORE he'd never run for mayor. He suspected it was filthy business, like an unwiped big rig leaving the loo. Now he was standing on the pulpit, preparing to speak, to preach to his converted. Not bad for Optimus; he had spent all of fourth grade worried about a urine stain. Right in the crotch of his gray sweatpants. A perfect circle where the four corners met and the stitches pulled apart. He tried to wipe it away and actual moisture came off onto the palm of his hand, right in the middle—where his handlebars had left a nubby little callus.

Optimus kept the inside of his little windowpanes mote-free. His mother provided him with vinegar. His sidewalk cracks were filled with sprouts of grass, but his vacuum had covered every surface inside. He only opened his door to let in his one friend, The Bear. Neighbors wondered why the two men would be such friends. Especially men as overgrown as Optimus and The Bear. They had a schedule: The Bear always visited for twenty-six minutes, about twenty-five times a year. He often had an idea, an idea that made Optimus say *I shouldn't*—always a good idea. Mayoral candidacy was a new kind of idea; it didn't suit Optimus in any way. Yet, for the first time, Optimus considered one of The Bear's propositions. *Nothing's going to change*—The Bear held Optimus's mitt in his own—*No need to transform your life.*

The Bear convinced him to do it. He said the whole situation would be MINT. *Agreed, but my problem is I stay inside.* So, right then, The Bear took him out for a ride, out for a conversation. Two seats, tandem: The Bear talked, and Optimus Prime was given no chance for rebuttal. The more The Bear talked, the more they had to pedal. They just outran the new tram at the intersection—a very close call. Optimus saw his future; he saw it glistening on the sweaty fur before him, the fur creeping over the edge of a tank top.

The Bear's primary reason for encouraging his friend's candidacy: puppetry. Optimus Prime could comfortably sway at the ends of The Bear's strings. The delicate Mr. Prime was unoffended by this suggestion, even impressed. *Perhaps I'll consider it*—his nod betrayed his steel face—*but only if there's a per diem involved.* (He'd watched his father work a deal before, when he was young. He could get Optimus a single pair of sweatpants at the bulk rate. Although, sometimes he'd have to pull the drawstring through himself.) The Bear assured Optimus that he'd take up a collection at the Gathering each week, if there wasn't any other compensation. Optimus left everything in his hands. He wondered if The Bear's visits would be more frequent now.

Daily schedule of a figurehead mayor (patriarchal duties informally eschewed): Mornings are spent at the public pool, circle-swimming, satisfied with the knowledge that the admission fee was comped. Brunch with a spork. The arcade doors are opened and a bucket of tokens provided. A space at the foosball table is offered and politely declined. On to World of Burgers (W.O.B.) for the crinkle-cut fries. The day ends with a reinvestment of the money saved (several bits) in Pay-Per-View. In the silence of the evening, the absence of an ursine presence is impossible to ignore.

They were all going to vote for him anyway. Your-Next-Mayor Prime stepped away from the microphone before he even tapped it. He let The Bear do the talking.

Alf

TRY NOT TO WORRY about Alf. Contrary to the word about town, she had not been sent to the desert; she chose to be left alone (just as Optimus Prime chose to be alone no longer). She lived right downtown, in fact—in an attic apartment above the alchemist. It was a wonderfully stimulating atmosphere where varied aspects of the town's hubbub were channeled to her. Her apartment was composed of vents, chutes, and shafts more than proper rooms. With that kind of access, she had very little reason to come down and see what was going on.

Early on, Alf saw the worst. She used to maintain a kiosk in town; she was working in a difficult industry. She was on the street from daybreak until she could hear the bartenders inside calling final rounds. Usually it was blossoms, but she'd sell whatever needed selling that day. She suffered often back then; her bones tightened and her ligaments balked. But she was willing to struggle. The pain in her limbs became so acute at times that she needed to be carted about. Still, whatever it took, she never missed a shift. When Optimus Prime's tax policy hemmed her in, she found new revenue streams. She endured a lot: her stands were knocked over, rain arrived in torrents, restrictions generally impinged, fashion trends discouraged consumption, and she was struck with common colds more often than most. Nevertheless, each fiscal year, her profit margin was considerable, several bits larger than her closest competitor.

It was a problem at home that had finally taken her from the streets. A fire began in her living room at midday, and by the time she closed up shop, it had spread throughout her house. She had been trying out new recipes. One called for a slow boil. But it turned out to have been a misprint.

Alf couldn't risk another complete domestic loss. Her books wouldn't balance. So she decided to rent. She scoured the listings for a new place. She searched *smart*. She'd live off the fat of her venture's liquidation. The classifieds came up dry, but her senses were keen. She was always on the hunt. One day, she was waiting for the alchemist to concoct a particular conjuration that had been prescribed to her. Despite the fact that she was thumbing through her wallet, counting out her co-pay, her search was still on. She hinted that a new home would suit her. The alchemist, filling a paper bag with powdered metals, nodded to the door at the back of his shop. Alf seized the moment and entered, following the stairwell behind it. She planned to leave the store that day with a cure; instead she stayed—with a solution.

Word under the tent on Tuesday evenings was that Alf was too settled into her quarantine to attend the Gathering (at least among those who would admit she hadn't headed for the hills). The Bear would neither confirm nor deny her whereabouts; he replied with only the huffy look of why-would-you-ask. He then whispered something urgent into his black headset.

The Bear did mention Alf to Mayor Prime on one very private, most likely tipsy, occasion. Certainly, it was a slow day—a town holiday or a snow emergency. *Alf*, he said, *has found her own epicenter in that attic.* He continued, *And I'll tell you something else, which neither you nor I might want to admit: she's installed herself at the center of this whole goddamned town.*

Chopsticks

THE VALUE OF A SIMPLE PAIR of chopsticks had been increasing steadily since the revision of the standard cuisine. The prevailing dishes around town were prepared such that they could only be enjoyed with a clean pair of chopsticks. But supply was limited, and no chopsticks were natively grown or manufactured. There was obviously a great desire to build a factory, but there was almost no room to expand, and Optimus Prime's administration wasn't about to shut down any of the conventional utensil plants (not even Spork Manufacturing, Ltd.). Not to mention, most of the proffered chopstick money was from the pockets of the biggest eaters (the Honourable Society of Gourmets and Gourmands), which was clearly a conflict of interest—not the kind of muck Optimus Prime and his people were about to dip their hands in. After all, he had only been mayor for a few weeks, and one of his stated goals was to never rise above figurehead status.

Mr. Greenjeans was importing a fair number of chopsticks to sell in his shop. Some people even suspected that he was exceeding his quota. They fetched a good price. The premium pairs were precisely arranged in a velvet-lined show window. They became the item-to-have in the early autumn months. Some people would gather in giddy crowds around his window to admire the high-end chopsticks; others would try to find a quiet moment alone with the display.

Mr. Greenjeans watched them from his stool behind the register and was charmed by the spectators' murmurs and sighs. But that only made him want to feel their admiration more intimately. One night, after work, he left his shop unlocked and settled himself behind the hedgerow across the street. Who wouldn't be tempted by those glorious chopsticks, free for the taking? They were the fancy kind.

It was a quiet night, but citizens strolled by at regular intervals. Without fail, his chopsticks gave them pause. But it took a special woman to actually check the lock. Her name was Belle, the very same woman whom Mr. Greenjeans could never marry. She nudged the door and it swung right open. She walked into the shop as naturally as she would into her own home. *If only it were,* Mr. Greenjeans thought. He longed to cross the street as he watched her caress and sample each pair of chopsticks. Her soft hands gently tested every set in the window, prodding and then grabbing a feast of invisible food. He wanted to go to her, but he remained rooted to the rich soil behind the hedge. Belle selected a fairly modest pair and tucked them inside her coat. She left the shop, remembering to close the door and set the lock before she did so. Mr. Greenjeans sat alone, stunned by the sight of his altered display, now centered around a glaring absence.

He could have stopped her; he could have saved her at the last moment. But he wanted her to have those chopsticks.

When he arrived at the shop the next morning, the authorities were already waiting for him, pads and pens at the ready. The theft was excessively apparent to the whole town, and the officers were visibly shaken. *How could someone steal something so valuable?* they asked. They took it personally; Mr. Greenjeans's chopsticks had become the pride of the town. It pained him to do so, but he admitted to witnessing the crime.

Despite agreeing to identify Belle, Mr. Greenjeans could not bear to see her arrested. The only idea more unbearable was living in a town where depravity such as Belle's was left unchecked. The sour taste of the theft, and her subsequent removal, never left him. Chopsticks' popularity continued to grow, and Mr. Greenjeans became a very rich man. But, at his own table, he swore them off completely. Eventually, the town phased out knives and forks altogether, but, even then, Mr. Greenjeans ate only with his hands—sometimes not washing them for days.

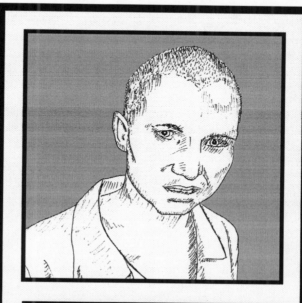

Gargamel

GARGAMEL HEARKENED BACK to the dancehall era. He was the very engineer of that time, opening hopping joints on the north side, the south side, and in the Blossom District. Back then, it wasn't rare to see him standing near the entrance of any of his dancehalls, tapping his foot, humming softly, a different song than the one pulsing from behind the closed door at his back. But he'd never stay for long—there was always another set list to write, a mathematical model to be built. In those brief moments that you saw him, it was obvious that he was a businessman, and it was obvious that he loved his customers.

There was a time when sessions at Gargamel's dancehalls were the brightest nights in town. Capacity would be long surpassed, but Gargamel's main muscle, El Capitan, might be found to prop open a back door, let in a few stragglers. But, as fate would have it, mayors came and mayors went again, each one leaving a new distraction, a new recreational legacy. More and more people spent their Fridays at the sack races, under laser lights, or breaking records of speed. Fewer and fewer dancehalls were necessary, until finally, Gargamel's last interest was forced to shut down.

The cops had let the dancehall stay open until the sun rose on its ultimate night. Gargamel had waited out the final set in the tall grass around back, lying in it, drumming his fingers to some unheard beat. Everyone who had ever set foot in one of those dancehalls had cried for him: *His time had come too soon.* But when the last record had faded, Gargamel himself wasn't sure they were right about that.

His real challenge had become finding a role in the everyday running of things. He got a job with the Town: tending official matters and running trips for the kids. He didn't mind playing his role, easing into age. He brought the ladies rugelach from EasyBake's on Thursday mornings; they cooed and called him king. Afternoons with his feet up in the sportshack suited him; he lent Frisbees and kickballs, and recorded the loans lazily. He didn't put his own calendar on the wall of the shack, but he was sure to flip the month on his coworkers' calendars (zeppelins for Willy Joe and llamas for Tank) every thirty days or so. If he saw the sprinklers outside his window pop up off schedule, he put in a call to maintenance.

On Saturdays in August, Gargamel led the ten-to twelve-year-olds on excursions to the carousel by the bay. Round and round, then a cotton candy and a dip in the drink. The Bear had gone on one of these Saturday trips as a kid, and, when he arrived home—even after the forty-five-minute van ride back to downtown—he was still crying. The gray Gargamel told his parents, and later the board, that The Bear was *inconsolable*. Forums convened behind closed doors and Gargamel waited at home drinking herbal tea at a furious rate. When the verdict was handed down, he was out of a job. They told him if he kept quiet, severance would be paid and details wouldn't be disclosed. He wished they had at least discussed the matters with him.

As an adult, The Bear shouldered many responsibilities as the-man-behind-the-mayor. He now had access to the *Sears WishBook* and in it he found the address of the complex where Gargamel was living. He dropped a note to the boys in landscaping. Every Thursday morning from then on, Gargamel's lawn was shorn and his beds were turned. Tuesday nights under the tent, an empty seat remained in the first row. When people asked if the seat was taken, The Bear always said it was. He would always say, *That seat's reserved for Gargamel.*

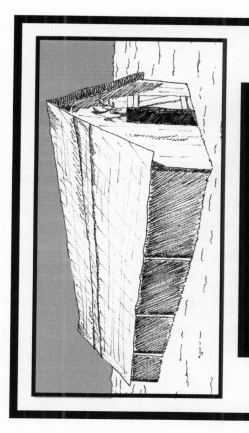

The Hall

THE HALL WAS just as you'd expect, everything as it should be. It was each of the following: long, festive, well equipped. The Hall was not a place you admitted to visiting. But, when the door was lifted—*just for you*—you checked your top hat or crash helmet and left the kid a buck. You wanted to be drunk in and swilled around until you were lukewarm and cozy. There were corners all over the Hall, and those interstices were where the living went down.

One night, a group entered . . . inhaled . . . and promptly exploded. Every single one of them. It was an unadulterated mess. Punky Brewster, who was sitting at the counter, watched the whole thing, but she didn't say a blessed word. And Optimus Prime was there (The Bear watching his left side, as he always did when the mayor was out too late) and no one said a word—about that. The clerk threatened to close up shop, but everyone knew better than to trust him. He just shoved his tip jar toward the crowd and manned his post. The regular customers traded sidelong glances and smiled. The clerk couldn't share the things he felt about the darkness he saw in the Hall every night, but he promised himself that closing time would be severe that night. There had been a terrible explosion on his watch, and those responsible would be made to respond. When he rang the final bell, several patrons were left behind—some to account, others to atone.

A lineup of the top suspects was called and the clerk's staff set to work. One potato, two potatoes, three potatoes—they were all there. *Now that we're gathered,* the clerk offered. *Who's going to pay for all of this?* his chief chimed in, thrusting a long, straight finger at the mess. Guilty silence was broken by a rustle from the nether rafters. Down dropped a pigeon and a squirrel. They ran and, of course, the squirrel beat the bird. The rodent was awarded the only exit. The bird was left to fly headlong, again and again, into the sash that had fallen shut.

I know how to settle this! Punky Brewster said, still at the counter, polishing off her final round. *It'll be a race. A free-for-all to the ends!* The clerk and his chief called a huddle. They decided a race would definitely determine who was responsible. The two men shook hands, and their staff added a chorus of nods (no gusto was spared). The lineup riffled.

On your marks, getset . . . BOOM BOOM BOOM. The race had begun but nobody moved. The suspects were frozen—out of options for escape but unsure they could each outperform the others. Their only hero (his name was forgotten due to traumatic indifference) stepped forward. Nobly, he sent the rest home—safe. Punky Brewster had a few extra minutes and spun her stool around to watch. Fellow suspects absolved, the man faced first the clerk and then his chief. *Are we ready?* They nodded. *You know what you have to do,* the man was told. *More than you know,* he replied.

The guilty party began to run his course. From beside his table he glided north to the mirrors and made his turn. Then he paced forward, toward the Hall's origin, a direction as yet unplumbed. Inconclusive finity was suggested, and, hoping for proof, the late-night crowd stared, shallow-breathed. The man strode toward the unexplored section and he diminished, as prescribed. Away away away—cyclical physics set in—and then: an End.

(Nobody made a report. What happened happened. And how could they have known anyway? Eyes pregnant with emotion, all along the quiet Hall, and nobody needed to say aloud what they all understood; nobody needed to be told to hide their story when the sun came up—should its daily return prove true.)

Hacksaw Jim

LUCKILY, Hacksaw Jim could light a flame under the whole damn town. But, for a price. Pay him two bits and he'd strike flint. Results weren't his worry; starting things was. He was long gone before the fruits of his fire dropped from their tree. He paused just long enough to let you see those orange and yellow pinwheels spin in the glass of his rapt eyes, then he was far across town, enjoying a draft or an espresso by the time the spectators were coughing and the soot began to settle on their cheeks. Later in the evening—on occasion—he'd sneak a peak at the horizon to see if a bird had responded to his call. He told himself that he didn't care if it never came, reasoning that it was good enough to have beckoned it with his flames.

Late on one particular Tuesday morning, crackling booms slowly drew Hacksaw Jim from his sleep. Peeling back his shade just so, he glimpsed the park below—all tar, no terrain. An old man on his bicycle drew circles, so tight he almost tipped. Almost, until he was saved by the thick heels on his new boots. To celebrate the end of each little lap, he drew a single red rocket from his pocket. Lit and released, the rocket set out on its own to explore the depths of the teeming concrete neighborhood that surrounded them. Neither Hacksaw Jim nor the old man bothered to follow the path of the shot. Jim watched his newly discovered old man, and the old man tended his whirring pedals. Go-stop-go. Two rockets, three rockets, four rockets—shouts. Hacksaw Jim drew his shade on neighborly politics. Five rockets. He cocked an ear and found no more crackling booms. Back to bed for Hacksaw Jim.

On Wednesday (of the very same week), the rocket's report came early. Dispensing of a double check, Hacksaw Jim zipped down three flights to the blacktop below. The old man had honed his acumen; now he could pedal and shoot at the same time—no problem. Rocket refuse settled over the bungalows and town houses, twinkling dust decorating dawn-drenched roofs. The old man's tires ground gravel and his hands offered firepower. Hacksaw Jim commanded him to halt. *Cease your goddamn fire! Putitout, put-it-out!* His demands were fair; people were trying to sleep. But his true concern: losing his corner on the fire market. The old man braked as told, and, turning away, Hacksaw Jim nodded. But the old man had his own request: *Will you light this for me, Jim?*—he offered a wick—*I know you still have my lighter.*

Here's the thing: Hacksaw Jim only used matches—that was the kind of cold, hard fact you could put right into the savings and loan. He used Exact Matches. He had owned a lighter once, when he was a rookie. But that was an ugly memory he had put behind him. Hacksaw Jim was shocked to find that the old man was right. Early that Wednesday morning, he found the lighter, stowed deep and snug in a forgotten corner of his old pocket. He pulled it out and struck the flint. *Okay*, Hacksaw Jim said, *but just this once.* The old man held on to the rocket this time. But before he went, before the flame reached the fuse, he said, *Keep the lighter, Jim.* Crackle. Boom.

For weeks afterward, the fires about town were left abandoned, allowed to simmer, spit, spark, and molt. Optimus Prime told The Bear to ask around. The Bear, of course, consulted Hacksaw Jim. He found him out back, unexpectedly hard at work. Hacksaw Jim flicked and flicked his lighter, and sparks danced about the tinder piles that were disappearing in the dusk. *The wood sticks,* The Bear said. *Where are your matches?* Hacksaw Jim shook his head. The Bear understood and patted his back. *It's time, Hacksaw Jim. We've got a good package for you.* The Bear left him alone, and he stayed up until morning, striking the same smooth flint.

The Crash Helmet

THE CRASH HELMET WAS something they all could share. When worn, it didn't reveal man's inner truth. Instead, it spoke to the world around him, his community, his civic body, his town itself. It was shared by rotation, an intuitive one. Actually, a polishing and a rotation. When one citizen was done with the crash helmet, it was meticulously cleaned and passed to the next agent on the understood list. It had been this way for years, and Mayor Optimus Prime's administration saw no need to tweak the regulations.

Wonderful feats had been accomplished while the crash helmet was worn. Most public works projects were first conceived of by a head beneath the crash helmet. The whole concept of record breaking could be considered only if you were wearing the crash helmet. (For instance, if Voltron had qualified for the Games, the town would have insisted he wear it.) The greatest parties had helmeted hosts. There was a keenly focused drunkenness associated with the heft weighing down upon your crown and the leather strap binding your jaw tight. And the best thing was that everybody got a try. All you had to do was wait your turn. Wearing the crash helmet was better than being mayor.

The cleaning process was intuitively acquired; it wasn't like getting up on a two-wheeler. No resident could tell you, *I remembered when I first learned to clean the crash helmet.* It was something everybody understood. It wasn't rare to see a young child, after her first or second go-around with the crash helmet, walking alone down to the riverbank to clean it. The process was specific but liberating in its rote. First, it was rinsed in the river that ran through the west side of town, the crash helmet's inside facing upstream. The wearer was to collect a handful of coarse moss (a vigorous and nonnative growth) that could be found only along the section of the river where the water's velocity was greatest, and with this moss the crash helmet was scrubbed vigorously—an equal number of strokes with the left and right hands. Soap was verboten. Then, a thin reed was used to dislodge any stubborn residue from the crevices. Finally, the crash helmet was placed on a rock downstream, in the lazy part of the river, where it was given the afternoon to rest and to prepare to be worn again.

The crash helmet was always waiting when the next person came to pick it up—without exception. The haberdasher, who had injection-molded the crash helmet so many years ago, took great pride in his creation and would watch over it. Now that he was in the blissful years of retirement, he had the luxury of waiting by the river and observing each new person strap on his crash helmet. He still loved it best, despite all the other headgear he had crafted in his years. But the basic purpose of the cleaning process became apparent to him, and he strongly disapproved. His crash helmet was meant to be shared and to grow with the residue of time. But they were forcing it to suffer constant rebirth; the whole town had conspired to stunt its maturation.

He aired his grievances one Tuesday night under the tent. The Gathered responded with sympathetic sighs. Still, effective oratory was not enough to put an end to the innate urge they felt to clean and pass the crash helmet. They had great respect for the old haberdasher—he was *revered*—but the crash helmet continued its rotation, recurringly shiny and new.

So the haberdasher built a dam. He was a clever man and knew that at his age he could never win a fight, not a real fight with knuckles and knees. He couldn't just snatch the crash helmet away from someone cleaning it. So each day he would squat beside the river and lay stones, one atop another. Seasons passed, and, at the same rate that the river eroded its own banks, the haberdasher's dam rose up from its bed. Eventually, the river became just a bleed and a trickle at its most vigorous section.

The haberdasher smiled as he watched people dangle the crash helmet in the almost still water, barely a speck of dirt washed away. It continued like this for some time. As his later years wore on, he would take great pleasure each afternoon, watching his soiled creation drying downstream, revealing the lives of the town who wore it.

Rainbow
Brite

RAINBOW BRITE TENDED certain public rows, held the key to the city (she liked being called in the middle of the night when someone was locked out), acted as the parade's grand marshal, and, most important, organized the annual Poshlust Festival. Then, one year, she decided to go on vacation. And everybody was invited. It was a package deal. She'd fill a van—a bus—a whole caravan. Or—if everybody could get out to the airport—she would arrange for a charter. That would make things affordable.

In the days leading up to the holiday, she met Sheila at the Sip Shop to discuss Details. *Oh, Rainbow,* Sheila told her, *that's because you're better than me.* Rainbow offered her pure cream. *Remember, Sheila, that doesn't mean I'm lazy.* She went on to relate another party, talk about another *my ex-boyfriend.* Rainbow and this guy she was dating went to this place for some reason. Sheila left politely but quickly when the time came (she said she had to see Hacksaw Jim about a job). The mayor had just come in and was hoping to grab a Koala Cola. Rainbow Brite called him over. *I hope Sheila will be okay,* she let him know.

In this town, Rainbow Brite had twenty-six and some-fraction men currently claimed as once-her-own. Sheila, and not Sheila alone, knew that Rainbow would be lucky if four of these agents agreed to be implicated. Sheila set up a blind date for her friend, brought a guy in from the other side of the pass. A big guy—tough. Sheila paid for his train ticket and a meal in the dining car, in case things didn't work out with Rainbow Brite. She just wished Rainbow Brite would let her help make things go smoothly. Let her do her hair, at least.

One tradition that Mayor Optimus Prime continued to uphold throughout his tenure was calling Tuesday night meetings under the tent. So Rainbow Brite told Sheila that Tuesdays were strictly out as far as blind dates were concerned. She had a regular seat at the Gatherings, but no one would save it for her. Now, she was consistently early, even if she had a date that afternoon. When she was settled into that unfolded chair, it was the least anxious part of her week. Snug under the Big Top. The air always froze down there; it kept a tear burning in her eye and in the eyes of those around her—together they gleamed. Before the proceedings began, they distributed popcorn, and *nothing,* she said, *was more invigorating than the yellow smell of butter.* Last Tuesday was special, because last Tuesday The Bear agreed to announce Rainbow's vacation.

Sheila, two other women, and—most impossible of all— The Bear were collected on the runway when Rainbow arrived with the dawn on the morning the vacation was set to begin. They had been waiting together in the cold dark, watching one another's emerging silhouettes. They realized they were not there for Rainbow Brite, but they were there for one another (who were there for Rainbow Brite). It was The Bear who made the difference. His bellowing morning hack and sweater-covered fur raised the stakes, introduced the stakes in the first place. The trip was underbooked, but, with The Bear already dozing in the bulkhead seat, Rainbow Brite was unafraid to tell her girlfriends that the flight would cost a little more than expected. And she meant it when she said it would be worth every penny.

Lady
Aberlin

LADY ABERLIN GOT a new job. They gave her exactly one-eighth of the TV screen, the bottom left section. It was her own little world and she could do with it whatever-she-liked. She had only one directive—and it was a clear one—keep it occupied, all the time. She started on Tuesday and had already fashioned herself an oval by the weekend. It had white trim and a subtle fade. Lady Aberlin couldn't help but be proud of her handiwork.

Of course, she had hobbies and interests. But those would have to take a backseat for the time being. There was a time in life for pomp and sacrament—but this wasn't it. This was the time to get ahead, to innovate—to make herself *indispensable*. One Thursday, she created a real stir: she invited a guest. Another face was fit beside hers and together they kept watch on the remaining screen. (Who it was, people can't remember. Some swear it was Slim Goodbody while others will insist it was Voltron wearing the crash helmet.)

The station's mail room was swamped with praise, and nobody in Litigation slapped Lady Aberlin's wrists for not having secured clearance. One intern asked the head counsel if he should draw up the proper paperwork, *in case she pulls this stunt again.* The program director interrupted and gave his two cents (he was eavesdropping on his colleagues): *Let's let her do her thing.*

Lady Aberlin was riding a wave, but she knew that she'd soon have to paddle for herself. Sitting in her screencorner, offering *funky* translations, wouldn't cut it down the road. That's when she got into politics; it was a necessity. Things were going pretty well in those days, and folks were settling in. Maybe some tweaking or shifting—both would be welcome. She began with jokes, a quip here and another there. First it was during the tired hours, and then closer and closer until she hit the prime slot. Her humor refined itself into commentary and then, fatefully, into criticism. Some people breathed, and others choked, but they all tuned in.

Then, not long after sundown on a weekday night, she said his name, the one citizen relegated to the shadows by public consensus. She invoked The Bear.

After that, Lady Aberlin's personal life escaped her. Or, more to the point, the media—her media—took it from her. They reported that she couldn't curb her compulsive filing habits, and as a result, her gardener left her for a better set of benefits. She now spent her off time in her laundry room tending to her brother's old socks (the brother who went missing at adolescence only to be found polishing public works projects up north, under an assumed name). They were antique socks, at least. A whole industry emerged in her wake, and it produced a slew of Lady Aberlin re-creations. These she was forced to observe from her little, increasingly claustrophobic corner of the screen. The Bear never visited her even once, never made so much as a phone call, but his point was made.

Lady Aberlin scoured her contract for clauses and realized her oversight: there were no provisions for vacation. They wanted her corner occupied each day—without fail. How could she regroup with no reprieve? A plea for compassion was in order—no sense or numbers, but compassion. Her argument hefty and ready, she marched down to HR and asked for her days—free and clear. No wrangling was necessary, though. HR nodded and sent her on her way. Time off? They all heard her question. *Yes!* They stomped one another's toes in reply. *Yes, we think that would be best for everyone.*

Lady Aberlin surveyed the whole staff. It was clear; they all agreed: the time had come for her corner to be swept clean.

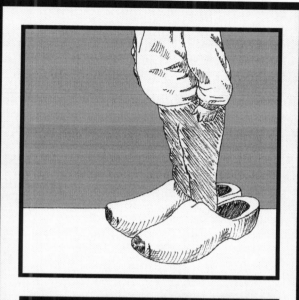

A Pair of Zips

TWO BITS FOR A PAIR of Zips: it seemed a reasonable offer. Word spread and lines formed before each of the five temporary kiosks that had sprouted up on the playing fields along the edge of town. Right at the foot of the hills to the west. The vendors hawked their wares; shouts were sent up: *Black pair! Blue pair! Size large! Extra-small!* The crowds flowed in and out and a community was born. Marriages were arranged, babies coddled, business partnerships cemented, even water sold. Some were disappointed when their end drew near, when it was time to make their purchases. With morbid charity they'd offer, *Wanna cut?* hoping for a few more minutes of precious expectation before the ultimate transaction. Blinded by ecstasy, the buyers always chose to ignore the salesman's wink in response to his sales-kemosabe's smirk.

Business had been burning for just under a week. Everyone stopped by to pick up a pair. Rainbow Brite cleared a cool half dozen. Then the five men running five kiosks closed up shop as quickly as it was set up and headed for the hills. The Bear caught the last one by the coattails and gave him a *Whatgives?* The man replied, *Managing expectations, m'man.* His compatriot salesman came to his side. *Knowing when to fold, sir.* And a third: *Leaving something behind. A red-hot iron.* The Bear understood the game; he had played it once too. He opened his paw and the captive merchant took flight. The quintet could be heard belting out choruses on their merry way as they absconded with the night—leaving behind a thirst in the throats of the uneasily sleeping townsfolk.

Lost souls peppered the playing fields among the foothills during the following weeks. But, soon enough, even this dedicated crowd took to staying at home, as necessitated by the heat wave, then the cold snap that followed those wonderful Sale Days. People looked at their Zips, neatly wrapped and ready for exploitation. But they had empty corners in their closets and free space in their garages. And these they happily filled with sealed boxes of Zips. *Another pair of Zips,* many of them said, *and then you might have something. But just these? No thanks.*

Voltron, Alf, and a handful more had second thoughts. They opened their packages, their plunder from those Glorious Days of the Five Vendors. Each was rewarded with a new pair of shoes inside. Voltron, for instance, tried his on, and the fit was divine. *Not too shabby,* lonely voices were agreeing about town. They took to the streets and people took notice of the new leather on their feet. An outside agency came in and offered endorsement deals, while this thing was still a murmur. *Get in there while it's still cool,* the agency's representatives were told. *If this thing should roll to a boil, we want our fingers first on the pulse.* With documents and totes in hand, the representatives flew, turning the fortunate handful into a gaggle of pleasantly surprised joggers and Sunday walkers. In exchange for their signatures, they were christened "minor celebrities" and "spokespersons."

Payments were made and posters alit in the likely spots. Voltron, Alf, and the handful more became the face of Zips. *Consistency,* the reps told their new poster children. *You are your Zips on the poster; you are your Zips on the street.* They were contractually bound, so they pushed—Voltron, Alf, each one of them. The campaign was embraced and savored. People rejoiced in it all, everything but the Zips themselves. Somewhere, the message set out on its own, leaving behind the shoes that had given birth to it. The agency sent a directive to its reps: ZIPS ARE A BLACK HOLE. Requisite checks were cut to the remaining endorsers and the reps cleared town, as the vendors had before them.

On their way out, they crossed through the playing fields at the foot of the hills. Five small groups had gathered, smiling to one another, twitching every so often when something moved among the hilltops. *Who are you?* one rep asked a man, his Zips tied tight. *A believer. We're gathered for the comeback.*

The reps hurried back to the agency.

Kiosks

THE KIOSK WAS THE STANDARD forum for commerce, where bits (the standard unit of commerce) were exchanged. Things could be bought and sold only through its medium (unless a vendor secured a rare variance for a cornerstore or a shopping mall). But kiosks became something more to those who built them—and used them. They were a way of standing alone, being an individual, while still abiding by a social contract. People added throw rugs and moldings to their kiosks, and Storm Shadow became the first to install a toilet. Once you obtained a kiosk, it was yours for life, unless you made the mistake of abandoning it, even for a quick breather.

Insomnia ran rampant among those who ran the kiosks. There was a time when people wouldn't talk about it, but kiosk sleeplessness eventually became the darling topic of the tabloid media. "Caught Napping" was a rare headline to read in those days. And the merchants inside their kiosks sought relief. Insomnia was a mild burden, but the microscope of the public eye was too much to bear. Their businesses became twofold: they sold their wares out of their front windows to passing customers, and they developed a remedy trade out of their back doors—with one another.

The kiosk dwellers became so caught up in their own challenges (i.e., their failed search for a cure) that business started to sag. Incensed by poor service, the town's Fraggle population boycotted the kiosks en masse. They found alternative systems of trade, going so far as to barter with one another. The tired merchants did not even have the energy to take notice. Their prices soared and they let them go. Most of them spent the workday—when they should have been hawking and catcalling—huddled hard against their back doors, listening closely should the solution to nighttime rest happen by.

And one day, it did. But, like everything else at the height of the Prime administration, it required government intervention. After getting word of the stir, The Bear sent an envoy to check out what was happening behind the kiosks. The envoy was disappointed to find what he had suspected: the back doors of the kiosks had all been left wide open. Toes were sticking out; merchants were thinking about leaving their posts. Nervous eyes peeked at him as he walked down the alley of open doors. Hushed whispers begged for z's. Vacant kiosks meant an end to the prosperity of the mayor's term. The envoy left, determined to find sleep, a sleep he could share.

It was decided that sleep could be brought only by force. The mayor's office accomplished it with a series of under-the-table deals. But the most effective measure was simply giving a few bits to teenage hang-abouts for their services. In one fell swoop, the teenagers slammed shut the open back doors of every kiosk. They nailed timbers across each doorframe. They sang lullabies when night fell. They hushed all passersby and encouraged them to join the chorus of numbness for the beleaguered merchants. Sometimes, The Bear was seen conducting vespers. With the aid of nighttime song, slumber returned, and, with it, a stable economy.

Slim
Goodbody

SLIM GOODBODY TRAVELED from abroad, because he had a job to get done. Nice compensation (including fresh pears from exotic locales) was dangled and he made his move. He wasn't looking for salvation behind the counters of the Blossom District or answers among the town's famous kiosks. He didn't think learning a new language would save his life. Hard work and nocturnal distraction—that's all he was looking for. He would spend his hard-earned bounty when the time came.

He never imagined the time would ever arrive.

The folks back home offered him free return train rides on a periodic basis. But Slim Goodbody said, *Forget it.* Even if he didn't know anyone here, there was nothing he hadn't seen back there. People around town began to gather this from his shrugs and silences. This guy had *memories.* His mind was *occupied.* People wanted reports of his experience, but no one had gathered up the courage to demand them. Instead, they let Slim Goodbody turn the tables; they let him level such a look against them that there was nothing they could do, except hope to clear their own names. He wouldn't scream, he wouldn't yell, he wouldn't laugh, he wouldn't smirk, he wouldn't even sob for them. He wouldn't give anyone the distraction.

In reality, things were hard for Slim Goodbody, not that he allowed anyone to guess it. It's hard to live in a new place. He had been warned (by his mother). He picked up a few phrases, but that didn't constitute intimate contact. He tried a new restaurant for every meal, but that only reminded him of his alien palate. He met a new girl (one of several), but he wasn't the type to let another person be his savior. If he ever did go home, there'd be no consideration of her tagging along. It was a treacherous line of thinking, anyway; it was dangerous to consider either that things might last, or that he might ever go home. The best thing to do was to eat something hot after work and then return to his suite—alone or accompanied; which one depended on the next day's workload.

Strangeness is lonely, but there was no lack of citizens lining up to be Slim Goodbody's friend. Some issued formal requests, but most let their intentions be known through the barkeep who fashioned Slim Goodbody his first after-work cocktail each day. The barkeep kept a tidy list, updated daily, which he showed to Slim Goodbody as he breathed in his first few sips. He nodded and accepted most offers, turning down the rare applicant for very personal reasons.

The new members of Slim Goodbody's circle enjoyed being there, but it wasn't long before they began to question his commitment. They wanted to live his adventure, see the world over the hills through his eyes. But he was tired when they gathered; he had worked a full day. He often didn't speak loud enough for them to enjoy his accent.

Slim Goodbody did give his friends some signs of encouragement. One Tuesday night he appeared under the tent. Many a man offered his chair, but he was just fine standing. His opinions on the issues weren't clear; he withheld even his signature nod on that balmy evening (his friends were watching). He refrained from weighing in on the public referendums. But his eyes and ears were attentive. He was becoming a part of the town. And that was a good sign, or so his friends told one another. Still, deep down, they shared a great deal of regret: their journeyman threatened to go native.

Slim Goodbody became a regular Tuesday night communicant. First standing, soon sitting, and, eventually, scribbling notes, sometimes furiously. And then he was gone.

His friends were bereft. They called in sick the next day (telling no lies) and, first thing in the morning, they went to find him in his office. They were informed that his tasks were complete and Slim Goodbody had moved on. One by one they stepped outside, and in the crisp morning light, they gasped and they floundered. They were faced with seven empty hours and all they could do was ask questions. By lunchtime they had a favorite: *But I really thought he was adapting, didn't you?*

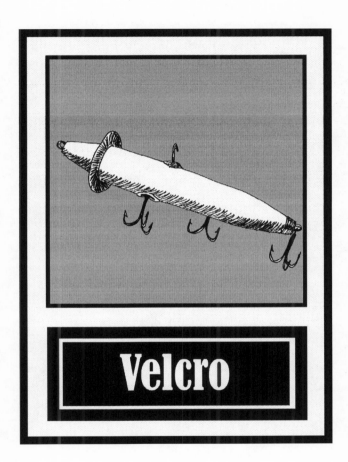

Velcro

IT WAS SOMETHING that touched people where it meant the most. People cherished their Velcro when they were alone—or sometimes with their immediate families. Velcro was solemn; it was usually found in kitchens. For years, people had been doubting if real innovation was possible; Velcro seemed so fully realized. It was admitted that change might come—but acknowledged only in whispers—between thundering knocks on wood and the grating dirge of the head side of a one-bit coin scraping against the tailside of another. People liked their Velcro exactly the way it was; they just didn't trust that it would stay that way.

Velcro was not dangerous, but every parent kept it hidden, because it was precious, sacramental. Velcro was a private institution. So when a man—a Stranger—was reported waltzing around the streets behind the stadium with his Velcro out in the open, an alarm went off. But what could they do? Was there even anything on the books to address this situation? It was so unlikely that someone would do this. The Bear's phone rang off the hook and he organized a committee to field inquiries. He couldn't find documents supporting action, but momentum seemed to dictate that he do something. A summons was drawn up from scratch (he couldn't make use of even a snippet of boilerplate) and delivered by messenger, and word was put out that the incident was over. The people, as a town, could move on.

But the messenger returned a wreck. Something didn't jibe. The man was still out there, behind the stadium, with his Velcro hanging out for the whole town to see.

He did not refuse the summons; he actually accepted it rather politely, offering no comment in response. The messenger had been prepped for all responses, but no contingency had been planned for a complete lack of one. The mayor's office froze and traffic did the same. Out behind the stadium, the Stranger sat down on the hot cement. This inexplicable behavior attracted a crowd. The Bear's worst fear was realized: people all over town began to follow the Stranger's lead.

The mayor's office fell victim to indefinite paralysis and authority ceased, for the time being. Meanwhile, Velcro was put to the test. It emerged on all the streets and even some rooftops. It was brought from the back of closets and put right in front of the public eye. The cards were on the table, and by sundown, Velcro would either be made or be broken. The beautiful invention was paraded around town and some onlookers began to cringe, but not a single person balked. Under mass scrutiny, each individual's love for Velcro endured.

As a chilled wind brought out the dark parts of the sky, people went back inside, leaving out their Velcro to collect their lawns' excess dew. The last of the crowd that was gathered behind the stadium reported that the Stranger held his position. They left him there, not knowing they would never see him again. He was gone by sunrise.

This allowed The Bear to set his office back in motion. They no longer had to deliver a response that did not exist. Affairs were in the same order as they had been before the Stranger arrived (they told themselves), and that was just fine (they told themselves).

The Bear walked the town's perimeter to make certain that the traffic flow was sufficient, and, perhaps, to clear his head. He enjoyed the abundance of exposed Velcro and thought that he might have to go and get some of his own. He was relaxed; the Stranger was gone. But, just as he turned up the path to his front door, his face fell and he stopped in his tracks—The Bear realized that the Stranger had left something behind: the evolution of an Institution.

Danger Mouse
& Penfold

IT SEEMED ODD that Penfold should be concerned about his friend Danger Mouse, who claimed to be the happiest man in the world. Why balk at such fortune? Penfold held his hand and guided him across the street, while Danger Mouse, with a head full of bliss, stared up at the clear afternoon sky. A motorcade roared up behind them and Penfold dropped his friend's hand, knowing it's the right things that are hard to do. Then, social propriety triumphing over moral understanding, he yanked Danger Mouse's collar and removed him from harm's way. Weak-willed Penfold no longer faced taking—for the first time ever—his afternoon cocoa alone.

Danger Mouse only then realized his near miss. He offered Penfold a polite bow. He didn't understand why a motorcade was necessary. The pomp seemed out of line. Penfold hushed him and complained that he was always commenting on pomp. Danger Mouse held his tongue because he was content (hence his claims of wild happiness). The secret behind his joy he did not reveal, even to his buddy Penfold. He was so happy because he had an *escape route.* The hills were impregnable, a fact the visitors' guides touted and of which town residents were ever so proud (along with the charms of the Blossom District). But Danger Mouse could get around them. All he needed to do was to craft a careful plan, work out the final details.

Penfold was happy to revel in retirement each simple day with his good friend. They enjoyed slow walks and browsing the sticker collections kept in private holdings. But the moment that distressed him every evening was when Danger Mouse expressed his desires. If Penfold understood correctly, his constant companion wanted to leave. That urge was a complete mystery to him. Penfold knew it, just like they all knew it: there was nothing for any of them behind those lush hills.

Danger Mouse believed everything he had been told; that's what drove him. He wanted to see nothing, to run away to nothing, and to live among nothing. He began to show up for afternoon cocoa with brambles stuck to his jacket and dried straw laced through his hair. Penfold didn't ask, but Danger Mouse offered. He'd been hiking the hills, getting a lay of the land. *There are routes, Penfold.* Penfold offered him whipped topping: *Nonsense.*

The next afternoon, the air felt crisp and the sky seemed perfectly settled. Penfold sat with a warm cup between his hands and waited for his friend. Almost an hour ticked by and there was no sign of Danger Mouse. Calmly and promptly, he rang the service bell resting before him. The waiter rushed to his side and asked how he might be of assistance. *Sound the alarm,* Penfold said. *There's someone lost up in the hills.* He knew more about Danger Mouse's reality than the happy man himself did. He would certainly be lost by now, off alone for so long, without Penfold's interpretive assistance. Penfold sipped his cocoa and whispered, *That's enough of this goddamn bliss.*

Stormshadow

STORMSHADOW WAS a wrangler. She could broker any deal; she could fetch any price. She was especially renowned for breaking markets wide open. Her kiosk drew the biggest crowds, and she slept while the other merchants struggled with insomnia. People could still buy tulips at a reasonable price per dozen because of her. She spent two seasons retooling the inner workings of the Blossom District, and that's all she needed—she provided a little supply control (some coercion of demand), and unshakable patience.

A woman like Stormshadow (everyone agreed there was no woman like Stormshadow) always stayed in the clear. That's why it came as a surprise that she allowed herself to fall into the center of a media blitz. An unfortunate media blitz. Things became so bad that Optimus Prime wouldn't risk the public embarrassment of granting her a pardon.

Her public life came to an end behind the hedges that lined her back fence, where Jenny Mews and the six o'clock camera crew found her hiding. Not so long ago, the shamed woman would have told the newshound to *fuck off* if she had so much as crossed her property line, and the game would have been over. This time, Stormshadow kept kneeling in the dirt, waiting as they ran cable to her, an oversized microphone dangling off its end. She squished a stinky orange holly berry she'd been holding and smeared it between her palms. She apologized to the microphone and asked if Jenny Mews might excuse her while she used the restroom. Inside her house, she filled an overnight sack and went right out the front door. She became one of the first to clear the hills beyond town before Jenny realized she had lost her exclusive.

Stormshadow's mistake was to stand by her people, her former key to success. Her best man Reggie got caught up with some of his boys from back home, and he came to Stormshadow, laid out his pickle. *That's some rough shit,* she agreed, *but you're one of mine.* She talked to some people and leaned on some others to forget some things. When Reggie came back, after his month on the ranch, she called him into her office. *You got your job back,* she said. *You stay in line, and this whole thing's behind us.* Reggie stayed in line; it was the second part she was wrong about. The Bear had warned her, but she thought she had it all worked out.

She found shelter with a Welfare Mother who lived beyond even the sight of the hills. After her escape, Stormshadow spent her afternoons dusting baking sheets with flour, helping the other women who worked for the Welfare Mother run a pastry business out the back door. She became a role player, but she never ruled out coming back when things got quiet. If you were to ask anyone who followed the story in the papers, they'd tell you Stormshadow's goose was cooked, burnt and picked to the bone. But if you could ever get an interview with Stormshadow, she'd tell you differently.

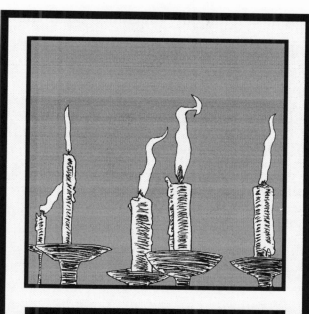

Switchboard

THE SWITCHBOARD WAS a bank of switches, little wires connecting one to the next, with a few blinking lights thrown in for good measure. You could flip a switch in someone's name, but never your own; it just wasn't feasible. A friend or an associate could do it for you, if he or she felt it was appropriate. Similarly, there was nothing stopping you from throwing all the switches that you pleased for the people you knew. The upshot of having a switch turned on in your name was that you would then be dedicated to a vocation—whether you liked it or not.

The switchboard was found just below the Blossom District, not far from the former canals. It was housed in its own kiosk, which was left unlocked at all times. A shanty village had evolved on the sparsely developed lots in the switchboard's vicinity. The people who lived in the dainty blue-tarped homes were not necessarily without economic means. On the contrary, they had gathered only because of an all-consuming zest for leisure that they each had allowed to fester independently. They zealously protected their free time and understood that the switchboard posed a threat to that. Should a known party choose to flip a switch in any of their names, their lazy days might come to an end. So, as a group, they responded with vigilance. They kept a watch over those who approached the switchboard's kiosk, offhandedly discouraging familiar faces, physically obstructing the entrance if necessary. In this way, they were never made to commit themselves—to anything—and they preserved their free and easy manner.

Mrs. Garrett enjoyed her time in the switchboard ghetto and didn't mind when rainstorms found their way through the small tears in her plastic roof. She was especially quick and keen at identifying dangerous parties entering the kiosk and turned them away with little effort. If it didn't flout the very foundations of her sworn leisure ethos, she would have volunteered for extra guard shifts.

One quiet night, Mrs. Garrett stood watch, lazily dozing against the night-darkened kiosk. She was roused by a small man approaching her. His face a mystery to her, she cleared him to pass. But he didn't. He stopped before her and reached deep into his pockets. Wordlessly, he offered her a gift, a token. It was a pair of wire cutters, the handles carved from hardwood, obviously handmade in the small man's workshop. Gift in hand, Mrs. Garrett immediately looked toward the switches, and the frail little wires that connected them, but she thought action wasn't in keeping with her lifestyle, and so placed the wire cutters in her pocket (as that's where the small man had kept them). He moved on without flipping a switch.

Predictably, Mrs. Garrett's patience came to an end. It was during one sleepless night following many others. She tore out of her shelter and ran to the switchboard. Inside the kiosk, she brandished her handmade wire cutters with fury. She was prepared to cut every connection, setting the town's beholden free. They would no longer be required to complete those tasks that others required of them. She slashed the air, left and right, up and down (even a few diagonal swipes). Those people who had come to the kiosk to flip a switch in the silence of the night fled in terror. When she had regained her composure, Mrs. Garrett gently placed the scissored blades of the wire cutter against one long stretch of copper. But she never squeezed the smooth wooden handles. Instead, she gave the tool away—to the next pilgrim who stepped inside the kiosk.

Mrs. Garrett turned her back on the leisure class. She still kept vigil over the switchboard, but now she hoped, for the first time, that someone would flip a switch in her name. Day after day, she looked for just a single pair of eyes that recognized her, but they never seemed to come. She began to consider the small man who had given her a gift one night. Would he ever return? And, if he did, would he know her? Could he flip a switch for her?

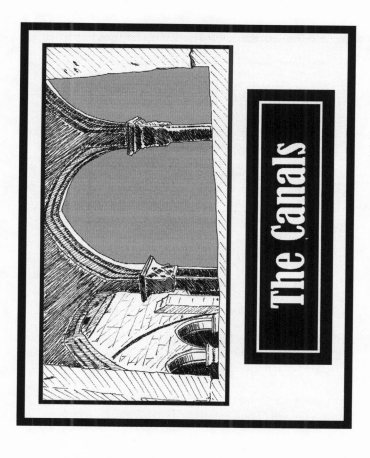

The Canals

THE FIRST HEADLINE of Optimus Prime's term was his sanction of a complete downtown revival. He would allow for deep digging throughout the area. Moreover, he would direct those shovels to dig until they struck gurgling, unadulterated water (and this was a time before water had been proven). Ultimately, it was discovered that seeping right into the downtown district was a web, a glorious confusion, of canals. The Bear, who by that time had been given the title of Optimus Prime's First Secretary, surveyed his list. Quality of life? *Check.* Commerce? *Yup.* Transportation? *Affirmative.* No downside. The Bear's censors confirmed what his intuition suspected: this summer was going to be the best summer ever.

So they threw a party—a fund-raiser to pique awareness of the canals. Signs were hung (it was a campaign): WATCH BENEATH YOUR FEET. And the project had a name; it was "The Canals Down There." The night was lit, the dress was snappy, and the conversation, as dictated by The Bear, casual—and cool. The Bear allowed himself an indulgence, a pat on his own back. He danced from first to last: the jig, the mambo, the Roger Rabbit. No breathers that night—he could read a demographic like a children's storybook, and, according to Benvereen, *That's all the big fella ever really wanted.*

I knew it, Rainbow Brite remarked as a stomping Bear passed her on the dusky streets of the Morning After. *There were jinxes all over those banks and under those bridges last night.* There was a hitch in The Bear's winning streak, and, in those early morning hours, the

Prime administration manufactured its second headline. The Dragonfly Incident developed stronger legs than most other tales around town.

This is what happened: A young Snork was sent home unescorted from the gala's closing moments. She didn't want to traipse, but it was an order. (Ask from whom and you'll get as many answers as people you ask.) She followed the canals; the maps with the fresh geography weren't due from the printer until the following week. Remember: with new water comes new biology. As such, this Snork met her first dragonfly. A boon for some, but only if you know what you're doing. Needless to say, this Snork did not. And, as already stated, it was the end of a long night.

Reports vary, but, put mildly, the Snork did not emerge unscathed. She was still alive the last time anyone bothered to check, but her condition was a matter of the State. The dragonfly was never found, even after a full sweep followed by a perfunctory dredge. Patrols were dispatched and the canals became a sad reminder, a place where people ended up remembering, when all they wanted to do was regret.

Blame was placed squarely on the Canal Project and all paths traced directly back to the stylish new mayoral set. Optimus Prime purged personnel and the censors were searching the classifieds by the next Monday morning. He called The Bear into his office and demanded accountability (almost unnoticed, at that moment, he acted as mayor for the first time). The Bear realized this wasn't his project anymore; he'd given his friend the name, and his friend took the role. *Don't worry, Prime,* he assured, *I'm taking care of this.* He wanted to forget dragonflies, but he needed the chorus to join in; he needed everyone to forget with him.

Years later the pavement downtown still had a certain timbre, a tinny ring. They all knew the sidewalks were hollow. Water was a failed experiment, but no one could deny that it still flowed somewhere beneath their feet.

Punky Brewster

Punky Brewster would paint the town whatever color you'd like, on any given night. She taught the kids their lessons—religiously—but they knew nothing of her postwork existence. She never ran into her students at the station. *Bifurcated,* she confided over a secure telephone line—*bifurcated.*

Her clock squealed midnight and Punky Brewster rose for the second time each day. This time, unlike in the morning, she was already dressed. Wrapped in a long sheath of waterproof, treated cotton, she stepped out of her side door and into the permanently damp alley. Over the remnant rails, under the rotunda, and ankle-deep in a rivulet, she found her spot. And there, she had nothing to do but keep dark and wait quietly. Antsy crickets and misguided woodland creatures completely overlooked her. She was safely tucked into the soggy shadows of overgrown grass.

It was a complete surprise that the hat-covered man should find her. Obviously, her location had been divulged. Hat band around his ankles, he appeared at her side. *A keen spot,* he said, and winked. *Unquestionably,* she agreed, *tell me one good reason I should leave.* He held out his hand, and on its palm: rice paper wound tight, around which brown string had been pulled taut. She opened her coat and placed it inside. He spun her around and it ended in a dip. *The Hall,* he said, *that's your reason. Unquestionably,* she agreed, and left the hat-covered man to hide from the crickets alone.

Late night at the Hall, and the schoolteacher was a ward of the state. She left her coat outside (she didn't trust it to be checked) and cozied up within. Punky Brewster always wasted the last dance to buy herself a few more precious minutes. Shuffling replaced silence and the lights came up. Ceramic and glass, soiled by the night's revelry, sat before her. She picked up a spoon and held it aloft. Down it came—mellifluid—symphony poured forth. The stragglers paused one more moment for a final bit of grace in their days, pushing off when her performance came to an end—with an expected crack and a crash.

On her clothesline, Punky Brewster left her coat out to dry, and inside, she finally found her pajamas: lingering, patient cotton. Blanket on high, pillow packed flat, her left ear sang and her right one buzzed right back. Her eyes rested on the window and anticipated the sun. And, against all odds, she was right; it came again. She was behind her desk, pencil vibrating, before even her most nervous student arrived early for class.

She-Ra

SHE-RA VOTED for the light rail. She was so enthusiastic about her decision that she camped out the night before the results were announced. Her camera was poised and ready when the proclamation was made: they would be building limited public transportation on the town's west side. She lived on the east side, but she'd have some time during construction to go house hunting. She rolled up her sleeping bag immediately and ran to the corner store. She bought a newspaper and a new Erasermate— all the tools she'd need for her search. She found new digs before the late edition of the classifieds was off the presses.

Living conditions were certainly a downgrade. Still, the extra rent was worth it for location. She didn't have a window, but her new neighbor showed her how to make one with a hammer and chisel (he had lived in the building long before the local renovation projects had begun). She chipped a neat square into the wall, from which she could watch the street below. The light rail would be making a left at her corner. She hoped she would never grow accustomed to the sound of its bell. She dreamed about it waking her up at night.

She-Ra's excitement drove her to exhaustion. She no longer had a kitchen in which to fashion herself a proper diet. Every day, through the hole in her wall, she watched the construction progress, until one day an actual tram came by on a test drive. Once she had glimpsed that functioning car, she stopped working and she stopped sleeping; all she could do was anticipate. Finally, the light rail's maiden journey was announced. She-ra bought the first ticket.

It was an icy day, but nevertheless, people showed up in droves to stand beneath a logoed yellow banner boasting: THE HORN BLOWS HERE! The ribbon-cutting ceremony began and the ceremonial scissors were unsheathed. She-Ra rushed the stage and asked the beloved mayor if she could have a snip. Shyly, he obliged, and with exaggerated gusto she cut the ribbon. A new era in public transportation had begun.

She-Ra decided her first ride would be to the town square. She might stop for lunch and then come home. But, as she became the first customer to settle into one of the tram's molded plastic benches, she knew she wouldn't be getting off anytime soon. She opened herself up to catatonia and enjoyed the ride.

She-Ra watched as the town square flew by and gave way to the canvas flaps of the tent and then, in time, the foothills themselves. She felt the tram enter its turn, and she was more than happy to do another lap, sunk comfortably into her seat. But the tram kept going forward, not back along its tracks. She-Ra thought they had reached the town limit, but the tram was pressing on, regularly finding new tracks and even cable to hang from and stations to stop at. Alarm wakened She-Ra from her trance; the scenes outside the windows seemed familiar, but she had certainly left home. This was not what she had in mind when she boarded. She considered barging right into the conductor's booth and demanding where they were going. But she told herself this was what she'd been waiting for; she had finally gotten what she wanted. She settled back into her seat with no hopes or dreams but to ride the rails.

Stilts

STILTS WERE MADE mandatory for all citizens. The statute that required them had no discernible author, but somehow the law inscribed itself in the books. And, these days, the officers enforced it—to the letter. At first it was one of those things that was understood. The law was on the books, but if you forgot your sticks, they let it slide. Now they were nailing old ladies and greengrocers alike, for minor stilting irregularities.

One night the grounds crew witnessed a scene. It happened as they were standing on their raised perches hosing down the west side of the town square. On a verandah that wrapped around a house on the east side of the square, an older police officer, slouched atop his stilts, rested beside a bright young woman. His eyes watched her from below lids that he could barely keep raised. Suddenly, she ran down onto her front lawn, with absolutely no stilts to speak of—barefoot, right out in the open. The officer tried to put on airs of nonchalance. Still, the grounds crew couldn't help but notice him bristle at the young woman's infraction. The young woman looked up at the grand officer teetering above her, as he balanced on her verandah, and the men of the grounds crew knew she saw the same thing in his eyes that they did: the officer cared for her.

The officer followed the verandah around back and stepped out of the grounds crew's sight. They sprayed down the last of the dust to the rhythm of his racket behind the house. The bright young woman crawled back into the comfort of her verandah and wondered if her officer would return. The grounds crew, as they rolled up their hoses in a staggered but orderly succession, commented to one another, *The regulations won't allow them to come together*. Not one of them saw how it might happen. The woman stood alone, still without her stilts, albeit less confidently, while the officer's clatters and groans rose from out back.

The grounds crew adjusted their stilts, but they weren't ready to shuffle away yet. The woman shouted around back for the officer to show himself—without delay. Instead, a pair of stilts appeared. They were brand-new, handcrafted and extra-tall. They trembled before her. Eyes blazing, she shouted, *Are those for me?* knowing full well they were. She peeked around the house and said, *Officer? Where are you, Officer?* Exhausted, she leaned against her new stilts and began to laugh. Shyly, the officer stomped forward from the house's opposite side, and, once again, both players were in full view of the grounds crew (who, seeing two people and four stilts, began to doubt their predictions of a doomed union). The rubber bottom of his left stilt nudged her grounded foot and she looked up—dumbstruck. *Let's go,* he commanded, and she pulled him down from his stilts. Together they walked off the verandah and onto the moist dust of the town square. The officer saw the grounds crew scatter, barely maintaining their balance as they fled. They would surely report him, and without his stilts, he did not know what to do, or even say.

By the time the authorities arrived, the man's and woman's shadows could be seen chasing each other down the backstreets of town. He teetered precariously, again atop his stilts; she ran ahead of him, then behind, her feet surely bare. While the authorities considered pursuit, the couple disappeared down an undetermined lane. Remaining was one brand-new, handcrafted and extra-tall pair of stilts, left unattended on the verandah, on the east side of the square, for all the town to admire.

Voltron

ONCE AGAIN, Voltron was the man of the moment. Matters were a bit too grave in town those days, and he was about to return from his sabbatical just in time to turn things around. Joe would nod to Sally on the street, or Bill would wave to Terry in the park, and it wouldn't be rare to hear one say to the other, "Voltron—he knows the score."

One reviewer described his return as follows (all the critics agreed it was a terrifically poetic remark): "Suitable for us to quench our thirst after perspiration."

Where was Voltron during the many months of his sabbatical? How did he spend his days in exile? He was studying methodology. Board was provided at a notable clinic tucked among the verdant shrubs of a prominent mountain range. He rented rooms at a nearby inn. Colleagues in his field suggested he was wasting his time, but only in cafeteria whispers and under the cover of drunken nights. Voltron maintained that his projects were misunderstood, that the whole was greater than the parts. Whether the specifics of his self-evaluation were accurate, his product was wondrous. At the end of his tenure as the clinic's primary fellow, he dropped a sheaf on the scarred teak tabletop around which sat the Board of Regents. It was titled "The Krantz-Haberlich Method" and it was signed *Voltron*.

Back home, there was intense speculation as to his whereabouts. It was a total and incorrect consensus. They all agreed he was training. He was preparing for the Games. Come autumn, the grounds crew would begin construction of the winners' podium. Come summer, Voltron would be standing on the block reserved for first place, representing the hometown crowd. *Top Banana,* The Bear would say. There would be no match for Voltron, his lungs trained and accustomed to the rarified air from abroad.

Discrepancies between expectation and reality prompted less than prodigal praise upon Voltron's return. He was accomplished in his field, and rightfully wanted everybody to know. But they had had other plans for Voltron; they expected him to be their champion. As an act of goodwill, Optimus Prime invited Voltron to speak about the work he had conducted up in the mountains. But his address was positively leaden. Those gathered under the tent that Tuesday night nodded and a-hummed assent, but each one decided then and there—perhaps out of spite—that the Krantz-Haberlich Method was something they would never use. Walking from the podium to the back door of the auditorium, Voltron felt their staccato claps in his spine. He was on his way home before Optimus Prime had recovered the microphone and was apologizing to his constituents.

When the long days came, and the town took to its sun-brightened streets to celebrate its victory in the Games, Voltron stayed inside. His mind was parsed and admired in foreign journals—foreign journals hot off the presses—that piled high on his coffee table. The absence of his athletic talents was forgotten among the fireworks and hollers outside. He shut tight his windows and boiled water for fat yellow noodles. He coated them in butter—exactly the right amount—the best meal he could make. If he was lucky, tonight of all the nights, they would turn out golden brown.

Glo-Worm

GLO-WORM LIVED within town boundaries, but it was difficult to call her a member of the community—at least for her final few years, the time after she learned there were opportunities at the Chapter House and that there was a sign-up list. She could never resist a sign-up list. She walked over to the Chapter House at lunch one day and found that hers was the only name committed to the list. She thought that she would never be contacted, due to lack of interest. But not one full season later, she received a letter by post, the Chapter House's stately logo emblazoned on the envelope. This was her calling.

Glo-Worm entered her new life alone. It wasn't always this way, but interest had been waning at that time. As people lost faith in the mayor's administration, they lost faith in vocations. The Team Captain, having a team of only one recruit, phoned in his instructions and training regimens. If Glo-Worm claimed she was too tired to do her rotations, he let her slide. He showed her only half of the requisite knots, and he didn't even quiz her on those. The only day he showed up early was on the day of her final exam, knowing that his program directors would be in attendance. Glo-Worm passed with Flying Colors; the Team Captain made sure of that. But the fix was in; there was no way she could have failed.

After she passed the exam and paid her processing fees, Glo-Worm was asked to sign a pledge. She was to use her new skills for the rest of her days. Her ultimate pursuit would be *contemplation*. She had two hours to say her good-byes. *Clock's ticking,* the Team Captain barked, holding forth his stopwatch. He checked over his shoulder to make sure the program directors were watching. They were and they nodded approval. But Glo-Worm did him one better. She reached out and stopped the watch. *Good-byes?* She slung an arm around the shoulders of one particular program director. *Those were part of my old life. What do I need good-byes for now?* Everyone clapped as the Team Captain reddened.

They gave her a map and she set out into the woods. A small cement burrow was waiting just where they told her it would be. She dropped herself inside. She was not the first resident; the aftershave of the man before her still filled the room. But he had made the bed and that she appreciated. She unpacked her few belongings and began to count. From the few things the Team Captain taught her, the one thing she understood was that the key to contemplation was vigorous counting. As she inspected her new digs, she found another room off the first one; it was smaller and wooden. And conveniently suspended by a thin but strong cable was a simple wooden abacus.

Onetwothree began each day. Then one morning she heard a reply. *Fourfivesix.* It came from above, from out in the woods. She popped up her head to see who was there: a group of day hikers, her old friends, in fact— should such relations have concerned her anymore. They gasped in joyful surprise; they had found their long-lost friend buried in the woods. Glo-Worm did not share their excitement. *I'm glad to see you,* she said, *so you can go back into the town and tell everyone I've pledged myself to a mission. And I can't be disturbed. Please leave me to my place in the woods and tell them all to let me be.* She went back down and picked up where she had left off. *Fourfivesix.*

Glo-Worm was pleased with the passionate start to her new life. That is, until her abacus caught fire on the candles that she kept for warmth. She wanted to put them out, but the Team Captain had skipped that lesson. She let the wicks burn right down to the colorful beads that she slipped back and forth each day. The flames came and she stayed in her burrow, pledged to her new life until it was over.

Her hiking friends made it back to town and delivered her message in no uncertain terms. People respected her wishes and her solitude. Unaware of the fire, the census-taker would step up to the forest's edge every season and place another tick on his sheet in honor of Glo-Worm.

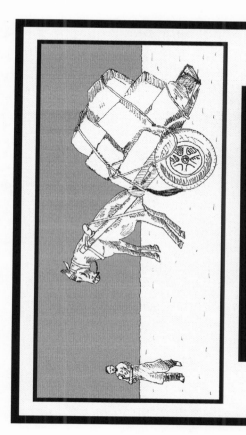

The Dining Car

AFTER THE FAILURE of the light rail, the citizens needed a place where things felt like they were moving. Approximate motion would do. People were starting to realize that the Dining Car was where you could find that kind of action. It wasn't a new place. Even in the days when the old part of town was still made of copper, the Dining Car was there. But then it became a Thing. (And, please remember, a Thing rarely lasts.) Someone appreciated
it for what it always had been and this person wasn't afraid to say so, and someone, under the influence of entropy, agreed, and that person let the cat out of the bag and another guy caught wind of it and mentioned it in passing . . .

The Dining Car worked just fine before things started moving. They were understaffed and loving it. They didn't have to pass code; inspectors came and went, but they were good enough never to call roll. Then, when business boomed, the Dining Car was thrown straight off its tracks. Crews inspected the rails and a sizzle could be smelled almost a week later. The grass behind it had grown unhindered for seasons on end, and now it was crushed. Inspections revealed that the brakeman was off duty. In reality, he had never been hired—ever. After the derailment, the cook spent a season running his business out of the back window of the Dining Car and kept watch over his abandoned tracks in the evenings. During these quiet times, he breathed with unprecedented regularity and thought about restaffing.

Deprived of automatic locomotion, as models would dictate, sales lagged (as did the Dining Car's celebrity status). But what profit existed worked for itself and soon blossomed into a retainer for a well-regarded hauling crew. Their services were committed only until lunchtime, and the cook prepared for their arrival. He cleared a wide path with a borrowed lawn tractor. One or two heave-hos and the Dining Car sunk into its familiar rails. Nobody washed their hands until they heard *click*. They did good work that morning, and the click came quickly. The fallow space now vacated, all agreed they had created a glorious new patch. The cook suggested lawn darts, and they played three rounds before the midday whistle wheezed its plight to the hauling crew.

With movement restored, patron traffic returned to pre-derailing levels. Expectations were met, and if one had the speed to pace the Dining Car's always open windows, he could see for himself. The customers were at peace. The issue of the brakeman was never addressed, and the mayor's office was being forced to take notice. Special interests had gotten involved. (Following the Dragonfly Incident, Optimus Prime could no longer afford to turn a blind eye.)

So, auditions were held. People from the mayor's office organized the process, but the cook was asked to contribute his two bits. As a judge, he felt awkward, but he had no choice. He was told, *This will be your man (or woman) so (s)he must satisfy you—as in, make you content.* So he took the whole day quite seriously, weighing each decision carefully, not allowing the event to slip into the pace of montage. The applicants poured their hearts out and he watched, they poured, he watched, poured, watched, poured watched, pouredwatched. And then, he delivered his decision, two words to the mayor's office: NO DICE.

The crowds kept up their side of the deal, and the Dining Car maintained its side—as it always had—without a brakeman. The margin was too high for the mayor's office to address the cook's insolence; they didn't have the luxury to risk media involvement. Life was precarious in the Dining Car, for cooks and customers alike. That should have caused anxiety, but the cook stayed cool. He knew trends would change; he'd seen it happen before. If the car held its track just a little longer, until the rebirth of the upswing, stability would return without needing to be told.

Jem

JEM THOUGHT she was earthquake-proof. And she knew that a quake was inevitable. She did nothing to prepare her own safety, except to check that the inside of her Freakie Freezies were still warm. The town vibrated at a very low frequency and only she could hear it. She didn't know how anyone could sleep, especially the people over at emergency services. *Despite their deafness,* she thought, *can't these people feel what's going to happen?* Jem wanted to stop the noise, so she roamed the town, fastening clandestine insulation (discarded baby blankets and loveseat cushions) to various ceilings and floors. Jem did what she could to muffle the sounds of the coming quake, to save everyone else the worry.

She began to lean on lukewarm cocoa to ease her burden. But one night her supply ran out. So she took to her balcony to get some air and ease the pain of her knowledge of what was coming. Her teeth chattered in rhythm with the pavement. The vendors pushed their carts home along the traffic-free avenue below, and the wind stopped, almost on cue. In the stillness, she could feel the history of the town below her, the vibrant canal life that briefly flourished, then died, and the rising hills that were once crossed freely. She forgot why she had come outside—but, as always, the rumblings in the earth's stomach were with her, the grinding of the town's plate against the outside world.

Since she couldn't sleep that night, she went for a walk and found herself in the restless kiosk district, the origin of the town's insomnia. She approached the all-night cocoa vendor. The man in the window laughed when she appeared and he said, *You're not here because you're a happy woman.* He leaned heavily on his arms and continued to laugh. He was drunk on his own product. That drew Jem in. She picked up a cup and held it under his urn, serving herself. She let it cool, holding it in her hand, afraid that it would spill if she placed it on the counter.

Everyone in this town, the man said, *they think it's easy to stay still.* He refilled his own cup. *It ain't.* Jem, of all people, understood. She asked him about the vibrations. Did he feel them too? He did not, but he couldn't stay still. He made her a bet. He bet her that if she came back the next night, his twenty-four-hour cocoa kiosk would be elsewhere. She wasn't fool enough to take such an outrageous wager.

Jem, who doubted that anyone but herself would survive the big quake, believed that this man, this cocoa merchant, knew about the insistent motion beneath the ground. The next day, she went to the market for her creams and powders, her cocoa ingredients. The stock boy told her that he also had been to the all-night cocoa kiosk. *It's sat on the same firm ground for thirty years,* he said. The stock boy said that he always trusted their cup; it was consistent. Jem didn't want to believe this; consistency was the last impression she got. The stock boy said that the man behind the window was like every other kiosk owner; he never moved. He had a bed and a toilet right beneath his register. He was there to stay. He spent his nights testing his mettle against the strength of his own cocoa.

Jem never returned to the cocoa kiosk. She hoped she could relegate its memory to that of an apparition. Just a few days later, her vibrations turned into tremors and she taped up her windows, comforted only by her unique sense of motion.

Game
Cartridges

ONE OF THE CLEAREST INDICATORS of the Prime administration's downfall was the standardization of format throughout town. The dust settled and the game cartridge stood alone. The Bear and his staff had thrived behind the smokescreen of competition, but with time, their machinations were brought front and center and the public became less interested in the glut of formats (some of which were clearly superior to game cartridges). They turned their attention to political intrigue. The Bear organized a response, putting Optimus Prime onstage. Before all the eyes of the town, the mayor feigned admiration for the victorious format and claimed to have believed in it all along. But then, he took the greatest misstep of his mayoral career. Right up onstage, for public display, he inserted a game cartridge—upside down.

The Bear thought it was best to confront his constituents head-on. He gave Jenny Mews an exclusive with the mayor, and that's when Optimus Prime made his daring confession: in all his years, until that horrible day onstage, he had never once used a game cartridge. Even when the other formats began to die away, he refused to admit the inevitability of the game cartridge's standalone status. He lived in stubborn bliss, surrounded each morning by the paisley wallpaper of his breakfast nook, refusing to cede to the realities of the lifestyle of the very town it was his duty to govern. At one point, Jenny Mews reached out and touched Optimus Prime's hand. Although her signature motion, it was a gesture she would come to regret.

The Bear knew the interview was a risk, but its complete failure was impossible to predict. Not a single citizen could reconcile the fact that the man they chose to lead them neither believed in the wonder of game cartridges nor even knew how to use one. His penitent tears provided no reassurance. A referendum was printed and circulated on the black market and a consensus of NO CONFIDENCE was reached. Still, according to their social duty and their civic pledge, the audience continued to attend Tuesday-night Gatherings beneath the tent. They held back their boos and hisses, but Optimus Prime couldn't stop himself from apologizing between each item on the agenda.

The truth of the matter was that Jenny Mews had a bigger collection of game cartridges than anyone else in town. It had been her preferred format since the beginning. Being at the top of the news chain, she always knew that game cartridges would prevail. But during the prime slot, she had caressed the hand of the mayor during his darkest hour. She would forever be seen as a collaborator with The-Mayor-Who-Didn't-Know. This resulted in a Conscious Boycott, and her ratings went through the floor. She was once the town darling, and now the allied consumers had sent her packing. If she ever hoped to charm audiences again, it would be beyond the foothills in whose shadow she had always lived. She set off alone, while a rerun played in her forfeited time slot, a box of her favorite game cartridges tucked snugly against her breast.

The Bear had ridden out enough trends in his time to believe that all was not lost. He thought that Optimus Prime's reelection was certainly possible. He even stood a chance at an uncontested race. So The Bear returned to his own chambers to spend his nights plotting a renaissance. Perhaps this was not the wisest decision of his tenure, as it was within the gray light of The Bear's own ascetic confines that his once keen understanding of the minds of his fellow citizens began to wither. When morning light told him it was time to salvage some sleep, he settled his oversized frame into his twin bed. The only thought that could bring him peace was this: despite the confusion around him, The Bear had never possessed a single game cartridge, and he never would.

Benvereen

BENVEREEN WAS undoubtedly a family man. But he had lost something along the way. He made a pledge to the most ethereal and wispy clouds, in hope that whatever was lost would be found. He still loved his wife, but he wasn't sure that that kind of emotion was the correct kind of emotion in the current decade. When he wasn't praying, he kept his eyes fixed on the ground, not far beyond the tips of his toes, expecting that an answer soon would be there. He became well acquainted with the town's highways and driveways, the walks hollow and dense, the covered lanes and exposed alleys. He'd sometimes flip a shiny bit into the fountain and hope that it'd settle the right way up.

His job at the Sip Shop (NO BITES FOR OVER 50 YEARS! the sign boasted) was his first and only job. That made his face well recognized around town. So it was quite unlikely that his wife didn't know he worked there, especially on the day that she strolled in with Slim Goodbody. Benvereen knew that she wasn't there to see him; at least her record showed that she didn't visit her husband at work. They sat right down in his section. Benvereen looked to his crew chief for a respite and was offered no such thing. *Your table,* she snapped. He set to it and took their orders. To this day, Benvereen still considers that table often, and he still is not sure if his wife recognized him. At the end of the night, he didn't expect a tip and he didn't get one.

Benvereen reacted to the incident. He began to make his own friends. He took up dancing on the side. Although many swore it was his true vocation, he refused to consider it more than a distraction. But he knew he was good and he suspected that soon his wife would catch wind of his beautiful, restless shoes. *You dance with such vigor,* his instructors told him. *Your feet are filled with such wonderful spite,* his colleagues added.

Finally, they had a recital. Benvereen left tickets at the door. He saw the whole staff of the Sip Shop clamoring for the first row. But the footlights blinded him beyond that; the rest of the theater was an empty black cavern. He never knew if his wife sat in the dark and watched him dance on that memorable night. And he never dared ask.

Hobby soon turned intolerable for Benvereen and he returned to living life only through substantive channels, like his trade. He sold his shin guards for half of their market value and exchanged his stockpile of balsa wood for a new apron. He was home every night in time for dinner, usually with fresh bread. Often, his wife would be there too. It was at the dinner table that he learned she was working also, refurbishing the old canal district. This struck him as interesting; her work was very similar to his. He told her to be careful of dragonflies—and he meant it sincerely.

What Benvereen saw at the Sip Shop that particular night, now many years past: his wife enjoying drinkable yogurt cocktails with Slim Goodbody. Slim Goodbody's face, famously inscrutable, revealed nothing of what the man was feeling, but Benvereen's wife was content. Benvereen had seen greater joy in her eyes, but such peace, he didn't know if he recognized. While they waited for their drinks, Benvereen served them a small plate of complimentary Saltines, belying the Sip Shop's slogan. Slim Goodbody pushed the plate across the table, and, as his wife accepted a cracker, Benvereen thought he saw their fingers almost touch.

8

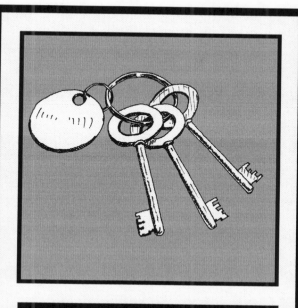

Party
Favors

ON FIVE PARTICULAR HOLIDAYS each year, party favors were distributed in individually wrapped plastic bags to all the citizens. There was a certain excitement in the air on that late summer morning when the new calendar of holidays was revealed. People riffled through it to find the five glorious holidays (one to represent each of the town's founding vendors) designated for party-favor distribution. If one of those days coincided with your birthday, you were in luck. You would receive gifts in multiples.

On the five holidays, duties were suspended and the whole town took to the streets to see what party favors they had received. They carefully broke the seals on their bags and peeked inside. The avenues and lanes were filled with *oohs* and *ahs*. Shop owners had the option to open their stores in the afternoon, but most took the day off to enjoy their new party favors. It was always a lazy afternoon and a good excuse to picnic at the foot of the hills. Even the garbagesweep reveled in picking up the piles of plastic the next morning.

Party favors needed to be distributed regularly because they had a brief shelf life. When the holiday was over, some people kept theirs, but most had nowhere to store them. Even if you did have a box or a shelf, the party favors usually found a way to disappear. Every few months, an infusion of new material was necessary.

The party favors didn't simply appear; their preparation was a precise and arduous process, led by the Den Mother. She and her staff would meet in the gymnasium on the eve of the holiday and set to filling the bags in an orderly process. They had refined their technique over time and now acted as a rudimentary assembly line. The Den Mother's bark was their ON switch. They moved in a slow rhythm lit by fluorescent banks of lights, buzzing high above their heads. The contents of an always full set of coffee urns fueled their creation. Sometime just before dawn, a few of the women would drive a vanful of party favors to a special kiosk that had been erected outside the tent. They would load it up so it was ready for distribution when the town woke up.

One holiday, the town was silent with the hush of morning expectation. All the people were opening their bags and picking through their party favors, designating favorites and candidates for trade. Then, a scream was heard just south of the town square. Papa Smurf had opened his bag to find it completely empty. His cry was repeated on the west side of town, just behind the kiosks. Rainbow Brite also had no party favors. Mistakes had been made. An opinion formed quickly: the mayor's office was losing its edge, and this miscalculation proved they could let the whole town slip right through their fingers. Some concerned citizens offered to share their party favors with Papa Smurf and Rainbow Brite, but it was a halfhearted gesture. Really, they feared for their own safety; it could just as easily have been any one of them who opened his or her bag, only to find it empty.

The Den Mother missed the daylight on that holiday, as she did on most. She spent each holiday sleeping off her all-nighters and the victory bottles she shared with her staff afterward. Usually she took an evening walk to enjoy the warmth of the picnics winding down and the sated revelers returning happy to their homes. But this time, when she awoke and stepped out, the streets were cold and barren, and all she could hear was a distant sniffle, from the vicinity of the Blossom District. She followed the empty streets until she found Papa Smurf sitting against a building, still clutching his empty plastic bag. When he saw the Den Mother approach, he asked, *Did you do this?* She reached down and pried the bag from his fingers. *No,* she said. *We filled them all.* She turned over the bag and shook it. *This wasn't our fault,* she assured the frightened man. *We had a system.*

Manuals

THE SLOGAN ON EACH MANUAL was "Read Once and Discard." It was emblazoned in green foil on the spine, a friendly script set within the neighborly tidings of quotes. Everyone received a copy of the Manual, but no quizzes were given, and in a short time, everyone obeyed the directions on the spine by safely depositing his or her copy of the book in a trash can. The result was one of the town's first public works projects: a huffy incinerator powerful enough to consume every scrap of leather and paper they fed it. It smiled and glowed like a jack-o'-lantern. The Manuals were consumed, the vigorous generation who had read them faded, and a new one took its place.

Papa Smurf identified a lack of order in the everyday running of town affairs, and he thought the only acceptable solution was a conventional system of standardization. He searched for a copy of the Manual, but they had all been responsibly discarded. Packing himself a brown-bag lunch, he caught the yellow bus out to the incinerator. He searched the structure from its hottest bowels to the outlying chain-link-enclosed scrub grass that surrounded it. The incinerator hummed quietly and worked as advertised. Not a single scrap of Manual had been left unconsumed. Papa Smurf had to catch the last bus empty-handed. He sat in the back, looking forward at row after row of empty seats, until he saw the back of the driver's head bumping along with the twists and turns back to the town square. The seat beside him distinctly smelled of urine.

All Papa Smurf had to begin the Reconstruction was his fleeting understanding of the previous generation. He consulted experts in various areas of the recall discipline, and with their advice, he produced a guide that he was just about willing to refer to as a Manual. The next Tuesday, he left a copy on everyone's seat under the tent. By the weekend, the Manuals had been read and trips to the incinerator had begun. Papa Smurf had not forgotten to decorate the spine with the same graceful words that adorned the original books. The town finally had a set of rules, and for the time being, its residents had a cursory understanding of them. As people returned from the in-cinerator, several of them disclosed the things they had read in the pages of the Manual, and inconsistencies were obvious.

With time came memory. The longer the Manuals lay burnt, the more their contents evolved. The town, as a whole, conceived of the rules they had read. Their un-derstanding was formed by of the lazy and the close read alike. Direct quotations (page and stanza) became less frequent over the years, but invocations of Manual-dictated policy increased. B. A. Barracus said it best: *This town's got some rules now, and hell, we're gonna use 'em!*

Papa Smurf ran into his old friend George Papadopoulos at the counter of the Sip Shop. George Papadopoulos liked to talk politics, and that's just what he was up to that day. The mayor's office was in disarray and he thought it might be time for a recall. He was willing to *lead an effort*, he said, as he took a sip and spun his stool, *but the logistics seemed dicey.* Papa Smurf delivered his old line: *Lack of standards, George Papadopoulos— that's the problem.* George Papadopoulos almost choked on his flex straw. He cried for the Manual; *But what about the Manual?* he bellowed. Papa Smurf took a seat at the counter and waved his weary hand. *If only we had committed it to memory.*

The Cookie Jar

THE LAST CRUMB had been removed from the cookie jar. The Bear had emptied everything into a brown paper bag, which he had then stuffed deep into the bottom of his backpack. Optimus Prime opened the refrigerator door to shed light on whatever other provisions they could find lying about the hushed and dark kitchen. Milky Ways. Fun size. *Count 'em and pack 'em,* The Bear whispered, nervously eyeing the whirring egg timer on the stovetop. *We'll need all the help we can get.*

The Bear grabbed the empty cookie jar. *Leave it,* Optimus Prime commanded, his last official order. *But, I said, we'll need . . . ,* The Bear replied. Mayor Prime put up his right hand. *Leave it.* He then held forth the palm of his left hand and on it was a tightly folded note. The Bear read the small print; it said: *For Jenny Mews.* Optimus Prime dropped it in the cookie jar. The Bear thought his boss was taking a clear risk. Leaving the note, and the cookie jar (and whatever else), meant the town's memory of them, the town's memory of their administration, might survive. *Of course,* Optimus Prime countered, *if we bring along these things, then our risk is that our own memory of this town might survive.* The Bear shut the refrigerator door, returning the quiet kitchen to its comfortable darkness. Optimus Prime opened the back door, and the pair of them stepped out into the night.

Together the two men pedaled, riding atop the same tandem that they had rode more than a year earlier, on the day that Optimus Prime agreed to run for office. As they glided past the row of kiosks, the merchants hardly blinked their weary glass eyes, not at all surprised or distressed that their mayor and his confessor were absconding. Together, the pair pushed harder and sped over the hollow walks that covered their now forgotten canals. They crossed the town square without even time to fully inhale and exhale once. As they crossed the path of the light rail, they spared no time to look either left or right. Finally they came to the tent—several stories high at its tallest point, but fully hidden by the stretching nighttime shadows of the surrounding hills—and together, they slammed on the brakes. They ditched the tandem behind the tent, as the only way to continue was on foot.

Their progress through the hills was simple and steady. Several hours into their hike, Optimus Prime paused. He had found Danger Mouse, curled up but wide awake, in the dirt beneath a bush. The mayor asked The Bear to open his backpack. He pulled out two cookies. The Bear protested; he said, *But we'll need all the help . . .* Optimus Prime held up his hand and shared his provisions with Danger Mouse. The lost traveler accepted his mayor's gift. While he ate the cookies hungrily, Optimus Prime and The Bear marched on toward the town limits.

Before daybreak they had made it to the other side of the hills, never to enter their town again. But sitting on the counter of Optimus Prime's former kitchen was the cookie jar, and secure under its lid was definite proof that he and his friend The Bear had once lived in the town, had once run the town, and nothing anyone said or thought could make the evidence disappear.

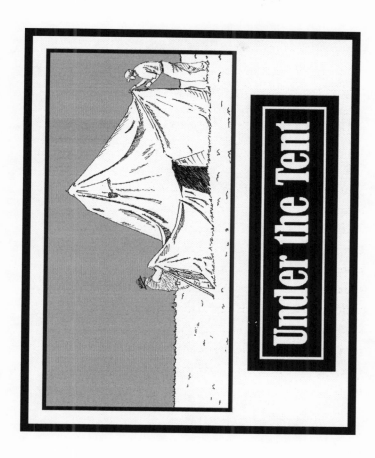

Under the Tent

IT WAS TO BE THE FINAL Tuesday Gathering. Some people knew it; some people didn't. It really didn't matter that evening, because the Crisis had reached such an advanced stage. Anyone who wanted to cross the hills could leave town as easily as taking a walk in the park. Optimus Prime, The Bear, and others had long since fled and there was no leadership, inept or otherwise, to speak of. Still, the instincts of those who were left brought the remaining citizens under the tent that one final time. They were all there when the clock struck eventide, no matter what panic the world around them was in.

A dais had been set up, and, impossibly, somebody had the presence of mind to string bunting along it. Of course, it remained empty, as the town no longer had an administration to occupy the seats of honor. The people filed in and settled down in their regular seats. Some looked high up into the tent's distant ceiling. It was obvious from the spots of black that the rips and tears in the canvas had grown large enough to let the heavy night sky fall through. They knew that the ladders would never again be extended to patch the holes in their shelter. As the final Gathering's beginning drew near, they noticed the seats of those who were already gone. Refusing to allow their absence to be so insistent, the people in the back moved up and filled in the gaps. It was an unseasonably chilly night, but they left the tent flaps open, should anyone show up late.

Once everybody had settled down, the tent was a whole and satisfying scene. The slight translucence of its canvas allowed it to glow over the completely dark town that surrounded it. There was the trace of silhouettes, people

173

together once again as a single community. And at the top of the tent's highest pole was a flag, a long, red banner flapping in the sharp winds. They had often said it would be a beautiful sight if they placed a flag atop their tent. And now, for the first time, the flag appeared, for their final meeting. It might have been an awe-inspiring sight, but there was no one outside the tent to witness it.

With everyone inside the tent, the town was a wonderful place to rob. The residents were hidden away, and the buildings and streets sat quietly abandoned. Blown debris collected unchecked in the corner of the town square, while the wind rattled the hollow walks that had once been the canals. The kiosks shivered behind locked shutters and under tarps pulled taut. And the hills stood still, protecting the outside world. A thief would have had his pick of bounty, should there be anything worth taking.

Under the tent, people waited for the session to be called to order. The time to begin came and went and nobody took a seat behind the dais. They waited for someone else to assume leadership, but no one had been left behind to do it. They heard a rustling toward the rear, and when they turned around, they saw a shadow slipping out. The exit had begun. In no particular manner, they wandered out in ones and twos and threes. The last few witnessed the empty seats left to calcify and hungrily enjoyed the final puffs of the tent's icy air. When they stepped outside, they were no longer together; there was no town to return to.

Epilogue:
The Roast

WHEN IT WAS ALL OVER, a group of them sat down to-gether to enjoy a hot roast. With their home gone, they had nothing to say to one another, nothing to share. Still, in regular turn, they speared the burnt meat and tried to enjoy it immensely. But their normal, natural routine of surviving from morning to morning had been ruptured, and they could not think of a way to approach the food that they had dragged off of the decorated platter.

The event may have seemed more congruous if anyone, even The Bear, had showed up to share a few words, to give a shape to what had happened, if Optimus Prime had popped in to reminisce. But they were left on their own. At one point, Hacksaw Jim asked Rainbow Brite to pass the butter. And she did. But he didn't have the heart to use it.

The roast sat, sweating onto its paper doily. Benvereen pulled out a brown diary and began to scratch away. No one thought him rude; they were glad for the distraction. His wife stood up to leave, and Benvereen ran after her, leaving his diary behind on the clean white tablecloth. Punky Brewster picked it up and began to write until her watch alarm beeped. Polite as always, she excused herself. Each person at the table, feeling the weight of speechlessness, found a reason to write or a reason to leave. The roast continued to lay uneaten.

Voltron picked up the book and began to jot down a few notes, a few memories. When he raised his head a few minutes later, he was sitting alone, just he and the cold roast. He stood up and the waiter began to clear the table. The young man had done a good job, so Voltron handed him a nice tip. *You're good at what you do,* he let him know. The waiter stood straight and said, *Oh no, sir. This is only my day job.* Voltron asked him what it was he really did.

I'm a collector, sir.

Voltron stepped out into the afternoon sun. He wasn't three steps from the door when the young waiter burst out behind him. Waving Benvereen's brown diary in the air, he shouted, *You forgot your book, sir.* Voltron waved him off and kept walking. He said, *That book isn't mine.*

ACKNOWLEDGMENTS

I would like to thank the editors of the following journals in which a number of these chapters originally appeared: *Beeswax, The Corduroy Mtn., Lamination Colony, La Petite Zine,* and *Pebble Lake Review.*

I would also like to offer my sincerest gratitude to my mentors, Stephen Dixon and Reginald McKnight. And I owe a great debt to all of my friends in Baltimore, Athens, Tokyo, and New York for their support and advice. Special respect to Ben Brookshire, Judith Ortiz Cofer, Brian Connell, Tristan Davies, Jane Elias, Johannes Göransson, Kristen Iskandrian, Kirsten Kaschock, Mark Leidner, Chris Luken, Sabrina Orah Mark, Jason Marak, Heather Matesich, Andy Moody, Mariko Nagai, Josh Parkinson, Claudia Rankine, and Jed Rasula who all helped make this book. Thanks also to Geoffrey Gatza for giving *The Complete Collection* a good home.

Most of all, love and thanks to Ginny and Nina.

ABOUT THE AUTHOR

John Dermot Woods writes stories and draws comics in Brooklyn, New York, where he lives with his family. He edits the literary arts quarterly *Action, Yes* and organizes the online reading series Apostrophe Cast. He is a professor of English at Nassau Community College in Garden City, New York.

3333112

Made in the USA